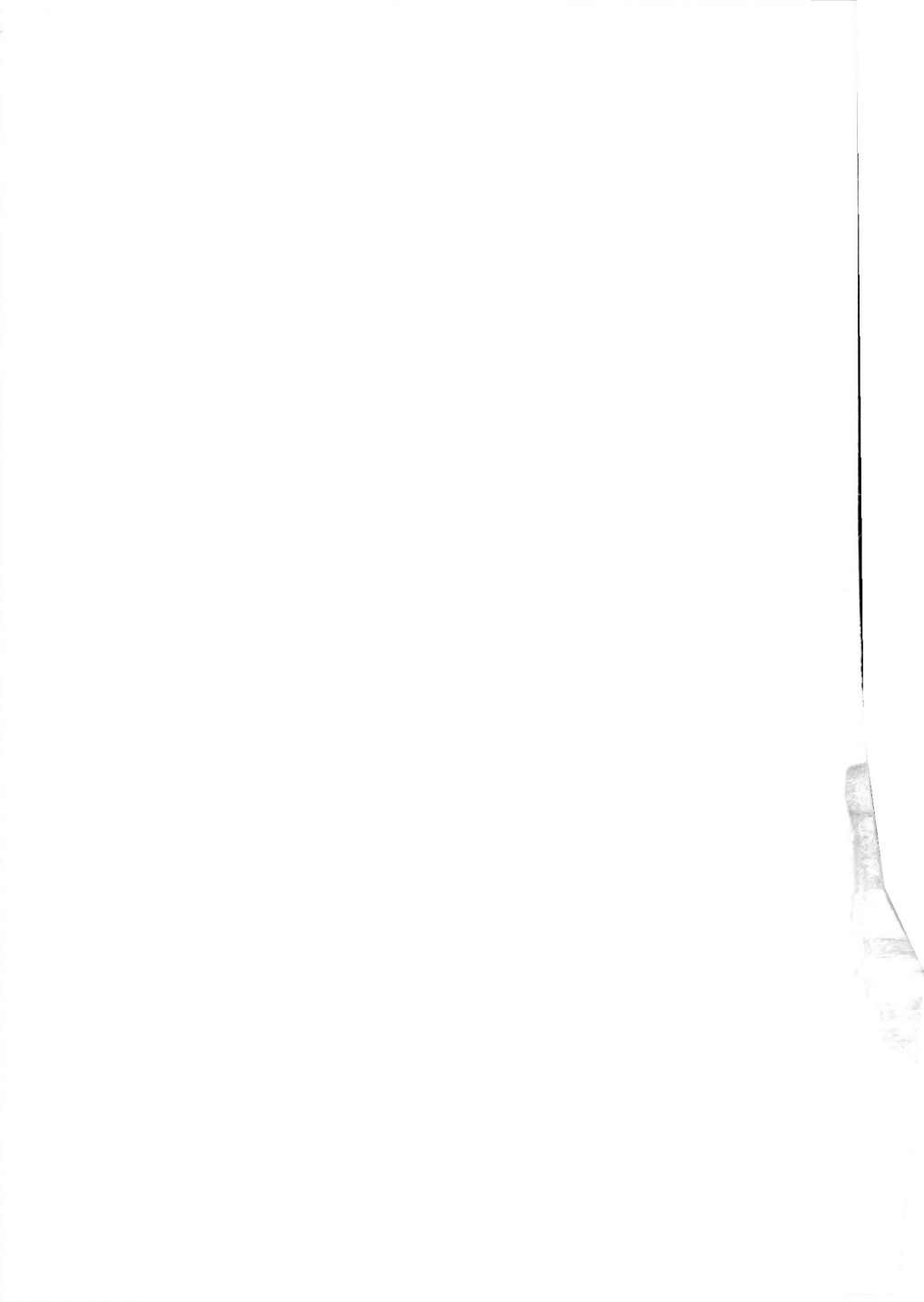

Smithsonian

DAVID DIGS with the DINOSAUR HUNTER

BY AILYNN COLLINS
ILLUSTRATED BY EVA MORALES

STONE ARCH BOOKS
a capstone imprint

Published by Stone Arch Books,
an imprint of Capstone.
1710 Roe Crest Drive
North Mankato, Minnesota 56003
capstonepub.com

Copyright © 2022 by Capstone. All rights reserved. No part of this publication may be reproduced in whole or in part, or stored in a retrieval system, or transmitted in any form or by any means, electronic, mechanical, photocopying, recording, or otherwise, without written permission of the publisher.

The name of the Smithsonian Institution and the sunburst logo are registered trademarks of the Smithsonian Institution. For more information, please visit www.si.edu.

Library of Congress Cataloging-in-Publication Data
Names: Collins, Ailynn, 1964- author. | Morales, Eva, illustrator.
Title: David digs with the dinosaur hunter / Ailynn Collins; [illustrator, Eva Morales].
Description: North Mankato, Minnesota : Stone Arch Books, an imprint of Capstone, [2022] | Series: Smithsonian historical fiction | Audience: Ages 8–11 | Audience: Grades 4–6 | Summary: In their long journey from San Francisco to Lusk, Wyoming, in 1889, David (Siu-Long) Wong and his parents have encountered terrible prejudice because they are Chinese immigrants; but here they are given a job at John Bell Hatcher's paleontological excavation digging up dinosaur bones, including an eight-foot long Triceratops skull, and David becomes fascinated by dinosaurs and resolves to become a paleontologist. Includes historical note on J.B. Hatcher
Identifiers: LCCN 2021030694 (print) | LCCN 2021030695 (ebook) | ISBN 9781663911841 (hardcover) | ISBN 9781663921369 (paperback) | ISBN 9781663911858 (pdf)
Subjects: LCSH: Hatcher, J. B. (John Bell), 1861–1904—Juvenile fiction. | Paleontological excavations—Wyoming—Juvenile fiction. | Triceratops—Juvenile fiction. | Dinosaurs—Juvenile fiction. | Chinese—United States—History—19th century—Juvenile fiction. | Lusk (Wyo.)—History—19th century—Juvenile fiction. | CYAC: Hatcher, J. B. (John Bell), 1861–1904—Fiction. | Paleontology—Fiction. | Triceratops—Fiction. | Dinosaurs—Fiction. | Fossils—Fiction. | Chinese Americans—Fiction. | Lusk (Wyo.)—History—19th century—Fiction. | LCGFT: Historical fiction.
Classification: LCC PZ7.1.C64472 Dav 2022 (print) | LCC PZ7.1.C64472 (ebook) | DDC 813.6 [Fic]—dc23
LC record available at https://lccn.loc.gov/2021030694
LC ebook record available at https://lccn.loc.gov/2021030695

Designer: Sarah Bennett

Our very special thanks to Matthew Miller, Collections Manager, Department of Paleobiology. Capstone would also like to thank Kealy Gordon, Product Development Manager, and the following at Smithsonian Enterprises: Jill Corcoran, Director of Licensed Publishing; Brigid Ferraro, Vice President of Business Development and Licensing; and Carol LeBlanc, President, Smithsonian Enterprises.

Capstone would also like to thank Sharon Lee-Nakayama, representing the Chinese Historical Society of America, for reviewing the historical content of this book.

TABLE OF CONTENTS

Chapter One
A New Adventure 5

Chapter Two
Bones Everywhere 17

Chapter Three
The Great Dinosaur Hunter 30

Chapter Four
Raising a Dragon 44

Chapter Five
Time to Go 53

Chapter One
A New Adventure

The Wong family was tired and dusty as they made their way into the small town of Lusk, Wyoming. Even though it was late spring 1889, the sunshine felt very hot that day. Their horse was on his last legs and desperately needed food and water.

"Wait here, Siu-Long," Mr. Wong instructed his son as they stopped outside the General Store. "Mama and I will go inside and buy whatever food we can afford."

Mrs. Wong clutched her cloth purse with both hands. It contained all the savings the small family had.

The Wongs had moved out of San Francisco when a third fire had burned yet another neighbor's house down. The family went to Wyoming in search of Siu-Long's great-uncle, who had promised them work.

On this two-year journey, the family had stopped in different towns on their way to Wyoming. Siu-Long's father had taken on many odd jobs, from farmwork to mining, just to survive. His mother had made a bit of money mending torn clothes and sometimes making new ones for the workers. Both had saved up as much as they could. They were lucky, in a way. They had no family to send money back to in China. So, all the money they made, they saved for their family's future.

"Don't talk to strangers," Siu-Long's mother warned, just before she disappeared into the store. "And let the horse drink as much water as he needs. He's been very good to us."

The boy did as he was told. He kept his eyes on the horse and thought about the kind man who had given it to their family. He wiped away the dust around its eyes and neck with the edge of his sleeve. He ignored the stares he was getting from people who walked by. This didn't seem like a very friendly town.

Siu-Long waited a long time for his parents to return. Finally, he decided to go inside. He spoke better English than his parents. Perhaps he could help them.

"Excuse me, sir," he said to the man behind the counter. "Have you seen my parents? They were in here buying food a while ago."

The man stared down at the boy. His blue eyes were framed by bushy eyebrows.

"I sent them out behind the store to sort through the garbage," he said.

"You want us to eat out of the garbage?" said Siu-Long.

The man's cheeks turned pink. "It's not all bad. And it's cheaper than buying produce on the shelves in here." He reached over to one of the shelves behind him and pulled out an apple. "What's your name, boy?"

Siu-Long told him, but the man found it too hard to pronounce the Chinese name. Siu-Long stared at the apple. His stomach grumbled as he tried to think quickly.

Then Siu-Long remembered Mr. David back in Green River. When they had arrived in that Wyoming town several weeks ago, they had met Mr. David while looking for Siu-Long's great-uncle. Uncle Lee had written letters explaining that he was a waiter, and his boss, Mr. David, was a kind man. He said life was good out there. But by the time the family had reached Green River, Uncle Lee had moved on.

Mr. David told the Wongs that people in Green River had grown to dislike the Chinese. They felt that Chinese men had taken all the good jobs in town.

Then one night, some men began making trouble for the Wong family. Mr. David advised them to leave Green River and gave them a horse so they could escape. Because of that good deed, Siu-Long and his parents were safe.

Siu-Long decided that calling himself "David" would honor that man.

"You can call me 'David,'" he said at last.

"All right, David," the shopkeeper said. He handed over the apple. David wanted so badly to bite into it right away. But he thought about his parents and stuffed the fruit into his pocket to share with them later.

"Thank you, sir," David said politely. He went out back to find his parents.

When he found them, they were talking to a tall, thin man with a wide-brimmed hat. He hoped his parents hadn't gotten into trouble. Sometimes it seemed to him that the local people were always finding ways to become angry with his family—even though they did nothing wrong.

As the man walked away, David's father turned to him with a large grin. "Looks like we've found work," he said.

David's mother smiled too. In her arms she held two sacks filled with old vegetables and fruit. "These are still good," she said. "We'll have a good dinner tonight."

It turned out that the man his father had talked to was looking for workers to help dig for bones.

"Like dead people?" David asked.

His father laughed as they headed back to their horse. "Not human bones. Animal

bones. These men are scientists. They want old animal bones that are buried far out in a place near Lance Creek. He'll pay us less than what I got working in the mines, but at least it's something. He told me we could live in tents out there too."

"And there won't be people trying to burn our house down," David's mother added. She wiped a tear from her eye.

David sighed. He didn't understand why people were so angry at Chinese families. His parents said it was because so many people were out of work and suffering. They needed someone to blame. It was easy to blame people who were just grateful for any work they could find. David had watched how hard his father worked. His job hadn't been so good that it was worth killing for, had it?

In Green River, David overheard a story about how a community of Chinese miners had been murdered. It had happened only three years earlier in a nearby town called Rock Springs. When the news spread, people became bolder in their actions against Chinese people everywhere. Thank goodness Mr. David had warned them and helped them escape.

As the family approached their horse, David told his parents about his new name.

"That was a good idea," his father said. "Best to try and blend in."

"Maybe you will be safer that way," his mother said with a sigh.

"These are difficult times," his father said as he untied their horse from the post outside the General Store. "It's easy to get angry at the foreigners."

"But I'm not a foreigner," David said. "I was born in America. And you even cut my hair so I would fit in with other kids here."

"That's right," his mother replied. She carefully placed the produce into the saddlebags on each side of the horse. "You are both Chinese and American. You are the future of this country. I hope someday people will come to accept all of us."

David's father sighed. "As long as they think we've taken their jobs, tempers will flare. If only they understood that we are all just trying to survive."

Just as he said that, a man with bright red whiskers walked by and spat at the ground just beside David's feet. David wanted to shout at him, but Mr. Wong put his hand on his son's shoulder.

"I read the other day that the government has closed its doors to anyone from China. No more Chinese allowed into America," David's father said.

"That's just going to make people angrier about us being here," his mother added. "Best to avoid trouble."

"Don't fight back," his father said.

David didn't think his parents were right, but he kept his opinion to himself. He tried to focus on the good news. There was work to be done. They would be able to save up some money. They would have a place to stay, and hopefully have good neighbors.

For a while, at least.

Chapter Two

Bones Everywhere

David followed his parents to the edge of town. The thin man in the wide-brimmed hat was there, standing by an open wagon.

"Just in time," said the man. "We're about ready to leave for the campsite."

As his father mounted the family horse, David helped his mother into the back of the wagon. Two other men were already seated inside, leaning up against large white sacks. They made strange snorting noises when they saw the Wongs.

"I don't want any trouble, you hear?" the man in charge said to the other men. They shrugged.

Turning to David, the man said, "My name is Sam Wilson. What's yours?" He put his hand out to David, who stared at him.

"Shake his hand," David's mother said.

An adult had never asked to shake his hand before. David took his hand and told Sam his name. He liked this man.

The journey to the campsite, as Sam had called it, took half a day. The ride was bumpy, and the afternoon sun burned David's head. By the time they'd arrived, David had fallen asleep.

Hopping off the wagon, David stretched and yawned.

"Is this it?" he asked. As far as he could see, there was nothing but grassy hills and mountains in the distance. The land looked

a lot like the places their family had passed on the way to Lusk. There weren't towns, or buildings, or even people that he could see. "Why are we in the middle of nowhere?"

Sam laughed and pointed behind them. "Let's get you all settled first," he said, gesturing toward some tents. "Then I'll show you the dig site."

Sam led them to two rows of grayish tents with a path between them. David counted twelve tents, each one big enough to hold at least four people. Sam showed the Wong family to the last tent.

"Is this for us?" David was excited that they'd have a tent to themselves.

"We're having a hard time finding workers," Sam said. "So, for now, you don't have to share."

While his parents settled themselves into their new home, David went out to explore.

On the other side of the tents, he saw a large patch of flattened dirt, about four times the size of the General Store in town. All around the patch were wooden poles, sticking up from the ground every ten feet. A rope was tied between the poles.

"That's our main dig site," Sam said as he and David approached a pole. "We have to be extra careful when walking in there. You never know when you'll trip over a fossil."

"A what?" David asked. He could see that some sections of the patch had been dug up, and there were stacks of rocks piled up to the side.

"Fossils are the remains of animals or plants that lived millions of years ago," Sam explained. "These remains are often embedded into rocks or earth."

Footsteps approaching from behind distracted David for a moment. His parents joined him. The other new workers walked up behind them. They all gathered around to listen to Sam.

"I still don't understand," David said with a frown.

Sam continued to explain. "Long ago, when an animal died, it would most likely be eaten by another animal, or it might rot out in the open. Sometimes, though, neither of those things happened, and the animal would be buried by sand and silt. We call this sand 'sediment.' The sediment would protect the bones from being damaged. Over the years, water would seep in, and the minerals in the water and sediment would replace the actual animal parts. The fossil is an exact copy of the original bone."

"What kind of animals are we looking for?" David asked. He tried to imagine a bear or a mountain lion being buried by layers of sediment.

"Mostly small mammals. But our main project is digging up dinosaurs." Sam took off his hat and fanned himself with it. He squinted into the distance. "There's a really special bunch of dinosaurs buried out here."

"What's a dinosaur?" David had never heard that word before.

Sam rubbed his nose. "What's a dinosaur? Well, they're just the biggest creatures that ever walked on this planet. They died out millions and millions of years ago."

"Long before there were people," David's father added.

David couldn't imagine a time when there were no people. Hadn't there always been people around?

"You know," his mother said, "in China we tell stories of giant animals."

"Like dragons?" David loved it when his mother told him those stories.

"Yes, and in Chinese the word for dinosaur is *hong-long*, which means 'terrible or frightful dragon,'" his mother said.

"And David's Chinese name is *Siu-Long*, which means 'small dragon,'" Mr. Wong said. David nodded proudly.

"I'll be!" Sam said. "It's like you were meant to be here, to help us find a terrible dragon."

David's heart swelled. He couldn't wait to discover his own dragon.

"This is where you'll be working today," Sam said as he led the group to a corner of the patch. "We're very close to digging up a full dinosaur skull. Our boss believes it's a special horned dinosaur."

"Aren't you the boss?" David asked.

"I'm just an assistant. The boss's name is Hatcher—Mr. John Bell Hatcher," Sam said. "He has an incredible sense of where the bones are buried. I don't really know how he does it.

He can 'read' the rocks. He went to school to learn about all this. I'm just here to make sure the digging goes smoothly."

Sam walked all around the patch. The others followed, stepping carefully. David saw that the ground had been dug deeper in some places. Most of the dirt was a light brownish-yellow color. In the middle of the patch though, the rock looked darker. David could see that the dark rock looked like the head of an enormous and strange creature. Other dark spots looked like bones.

"Are those—" he began.

"Fossils! Yes," Sam said.

Laid on top of the exposed bones were rows of strings tied from one end of the patch to the other. Another set of strings crossed them, forming many smaller squares.

"Why are there so many squares?" David asked as he pointed them out.

"This grid you see here is something that Mr. Hatcher came up with." Sam beamed with pride as if he was the one who had thought it up. "It's quite ingenious, really. We name each square, and when we find a bone in that square, we make a note of it."

"That way, you know exactly where it came from," David interrupted.

Sam grinned. "That's right. And when all the bones are shipped, Mr. Hatcher's boss back at the museum will be able to put the animal bones back together in the right order."

"Just like a puzzle," David said. He was impressed by how a simple idea could be so useful. He couldn't wait to meet Mr. Hatcher. "What does this dinosaur look like?"

"We don't really know," Sam said. "That's why this system is so clever. When we find enough bones from one animal, the people at the museum should be able to work that out."

Sam gave everyone strict instructions to follow. He handed out tools to each worker and set them to digging in different sections of the patch. They were given picks, hammers, and what looked like paintbrushes. They also got buckets and sifters.

David's parents were tasked with scraping and digging carefully around the large skull in the middle of the patch. The other men carried off chunks of stone and piled them up to the side.

"I have a special job for you," Sam said to David.

He brought two large buckets filled with a white liquid and placed them by what looked like a giant chicken leg bone. The bone wasn't buried in the ground. It had been dug up and now rested on top of a slab of stone.

"This fossil is ready to be packed," Sam said. "You and I will soak pieces of burlap in this flour and water paste and lay them over the bone. When the burlap hardens, it will protect the bone as it travels back to Yale."

"Where's that?" David asked.

"Yale is the university where Mr. Hatcher's boss works. His name is Othniel Charles Marsh. He studies the bones and sets them up for museums and other scientists to look at. It seems there were a lot of different dinosaurs living in our world. I can't even keep their names straight in my head." Sam laughed.

David had a lot of questions he wanted to ask, but he and Sam had to get to work. Perhaps after Mr. Hatcher arrived, there would be a chance to talk to the expert.

Chapter Three
The Great Dinosaur Hunter

Early the next morning, David emerged from his family's tent to find a man on horseback arriving at the site. The man was tall and lean, and he was just as tired and dusty-looking as his horse. He wore a dark vest with big, round buttons over his loose shirt and a hat much like Sam's. He was slumped in his saddle as if he'd been riding for days.

"Good morning, Mr. Hatcher," Sam said brightly as he came running up to the man. "You're early."

So this is John Bell Hatcher, David thought. *Is this what a dinosaur expert looks like?* He'd expected to see a fine, wealthy gentleman. Instead, Mr. Hatcher was just like one of the men working at the site.

Mr. Hatcher dismounted from his horse. Sam took the reins, tying the horse to a makeshift hitching post. There was a barrel filled with water by it, and the horse drank thirstily. Mr. Hatcher said something to Sam, whose smile vanished instantly.

"Now that is a tragedy," Sam said with a sigh. "I'm surprised you came."

"I had no choice," Mr. Hatcher grumbled, striding toward the dig site. "Marsh is very eager for the skull."

Sam jogged to keep up with his boss. David followed at a distance. He had many questions for Mr. Hatcher, but he also felt a little afraid of the tall, sad man. The two men stopped at the larger section of the patch, where David's parents had worked the day before. They spoke quietly as David approached.

Suddenly, Mr. Hatcher turned around and stared at the boy. "What's this?" he said, sternly. "When did we allow children on the site?"

David froze. Sam stepped in. "There weren't many people looking for work this week. His whole family is working the dig. He's a fit young boy for ten, and smart too. He understood your grid system right away."

Mr. Hatcher frowned as he studied David. David didn't dare to move a muscle. "You appreciate my grid system, eh?" Mr. Hatcher said at last.

David swallowed. "I think it's genius," he said quietly. "You make it so much easier for scientists to put the animal back together again."

Mr. Hatcher huffed. It sounded like a laugh and a cough at the same time. "Now if only those scientists would appreciate my work as much as you do."

David opened his mouth to ask more questions, but Sam gave him a look. That told David that this wasn't a good time. So, David ran back to his family. He was eager to tell them he'd met their famous boss.

That day, Mr. Hatcher hovered over the adults as they continued to work on what he said was the "very special skull." David was not allowed near it, which disappointed him. He was given the task of placing tiny fossils into a large packing can. These fossils looked like small bird bones, and some were even teeth. David's job was to wrap each bone in cotton and place it carefully into the can. It took him half the day to pack them away.

When he was done, David walked over to

watch his parents work. There, in the ground, was an enormous fossil, bigger than his whole family lying down side by side.

The fossil was clearly the skull of a giant creature. The top half of the mouth was long and pointy. It reminded David of a bird's beak. The beak seemed to split into two parts, and the top half curled upward. The bottom section of the jaw had broken off and was lying nearby, no longer attached. A large horned bone jutted out just above the eye socket, and behind that was a bony fan-like section. That part was what fascinated David the most.

"Be very careful," Mr. Hatcher called out to the workers. He looked up and saw David watching. He waved for the boy to come closer. David climbed down, careful not to step on any bones.

"David, have you ever seen anything so beautiful?" Mr. Hatcher asked. He stooped and

stroked a section of the skull that looked like the fan. "Look at the detail on this bone. It's been so well preserved over millions of years."

"What is this dinosaur called?"

Mr. Hatcher slid his hand over one of the pointy horns. "Marsh, the man I work for, believes these are parts of a large and unusual animal called '*Bison alticornis.*'" He moved back to the fan-like section. "But I believe Marsh is wrong. See the giant collar that covers its neck? It's called a frill."

David marveled at the frill. It was as wide as his father was tall.

"The horns appear to grow out of the back of the skull, at the base of the frill. That would mean this creature is a Ceratopsian."

"Ceratopsian." David rolled the word over his tongue.

"*Ceratops* is Latin for 'horn face,'" said Mr. Hatcher.

David's parents smiled as they kept working. David desperately wanted to say something clever.

"I . . . er . . . I finished with the small bones, sir," David stammered.

"That's excellent," Mr. Hatcher said, looking back between David and the skull. "Come with me."

Mr. Hatcher led David to the other side of the patch, around a small hill. David gathered up his courage to begin asking his questions.

"Why do you want these small teeth and bones when you have such a great giant fossil in the patch?"

Mr. Hatcher rubbed the stubble on his chin. "When dinosaurs lived on Earth, they were so big that most mammals couldn't grow very large. Not like the mammals we have today. Paleontologists want to study more about how those mammals survived."

"What's a pale-on—?" David couldn't say the word.

"Paleontologists are scientists who study dinosaurs, plants, and animals that lived back then."

"So, these small bones must be important," David said.

Mr. Hatcher laughed. "They are as valuable as gold. Museums everywhere want them to study and put on display." He rubbed the fingers on his left hand, as if he were in pain. "I've spent many years on my hands and knees, digging through sand to find these tiny fossils. But then I discovered a much easier way to collect them."

Before David could ask what easier way, Mr. Hatcher stopped and pointed to the land beyond them.

David stared. He didn't know what he was looking at.

Mr. Hatcher sighed. "Anthills," he said. He walked up to a small mound of dirt. "This is a harvester anthill."

David stooped down to get a closer look. Sure enough, the mound of dirt was a busy place. Tiny orange-red ants crawled in and out of holes. Mr. Hatcher explained how he'd discovered that ants were excellent collectors of tiny things—like fossilized teeth and small mammal bones.

"I began finding bones by sifting the anthill sand through a baker's flour sifter," he said. "With this method we can collect a goodly number of mammal teeth."

David reached out to try to touch the ants. Mr. Hatcher pulled him back.

"The ant bite is fiercely painful," he said. "When sifting through their hills, I find it safer to place a part of my lunch on one side, to distract the ants from what I need. With

this method, I have frequently secured two hundred to three hundred teeth and bones from one anthill."

David watched the ants. "How clever! You really are a genius."

Mr. Hatcher laughed again, but it wasn't a happy laugh. He pulled his hat off and fanned himself with it. David stood up quietly and watched the tiny ants scurry everywhere. Mr. Hatcher placed his hand on David's head.

"Thank you for those kind words," he said.

There was a long moment of silence between them. David could feel Mr. Hatcher's sadness and wondered where it came from.

Then Mr. Hatcher inhaled and spoke. "I'm thinking that it may be simpler to shovel the entire anthill into a box and send it back to the museum. Let the scientists there sift out the bones. It would give us more time to look for the larger fossils. But for today, I'd like you to try to find more tiny bones. Sift the sand until there are large pieces left behind. Then show those to Sam until you learn to identify bones and teeth."

Mr. Hatcher showed David where to find the sifters and set him to work at anthills for the rest of the day.

That evening, an exhausted David joined his parents in their tent. As he stepped inside, he overheard his mother telling his father about Mr. Hatcher.

"His baby son was ill for a long time," said his mother. "He died a few weeks ago. It's no wonder the man is so sad."

"How tragic," his father added.

"He's had to leave his wife all alone with this burden," she said.

"A man has to make a living," his father replied.

David's mother beckoned him to come sit

next to her. She hugged him for a long time. "Life is difficult, no matter which country we live in. But I am grateful for my little family."

David's father sighed and then brightened a little. "At least the men in this camp are kind to us. We are all doing hard work, even though the pay is not much."

David's mother laid out the food she'd cooked. She'd shared her produce with the other workers and, in turn, they'd given the Wongs some of their food too.

"Very soon, we will be raising that giant bone we've been digging out," his father said as he took a bite of boiled cabbage. "Siu-Long, I'm sure that will be a once-in-a-lifetime spectacle for you."

That cheered David up. He couldn't wait for the day when he could watch a "dragon" being unearthed.

Chapter Four

Raising a Dragon

For the next several weeks, David rose with the sun, just like everyone else in the camp. They worked long hours, doing much the same thing each day. Digging for fossils was slow and tiring work. But David didn't mind. As all the workers got to know each other, they got along better. They grew friendlier as time went by, and it helped that everyone had enough food to eat.

As summer arrived, so did days of rain. Digging and sifting were almost impossible on those days, so everyone was tasked with helping to pack the fossils into wooden crates. David would pack his small bones and teeth into large cans. Then, wagons would arrive to take the crates away for shipping to the museums back east.

On days when it rained hard, David noticed that Mr. Hatcher would stay inside his tent.

"He suffers from rheumatism," his mother told him. "It must be very painful, especially on rainy days."

"What's 'room-a—tiz?'" David asked.

His mother sighed, as if she were thinking of Mr. Hatcher's pain. "It is when the joints in your hands or feet are stiff and painful. It is an illness that is common to many, especially the elderly. It's such a pity that he has to suffer with this condition at such a young age."

David didn't think of Mr. Hatcher as a young man, but started watching him more carefully. He noticed that Mr. Hatcher often touched his hands. He was also often grumpy. David imagined that he, too, would be pretty grumpy if his body hurt all the time.

Toward the end of June, the days stretched out longer, and the sun shone bright. The weather grew warmer, and the work became more tedious. David had a feeling that the work would soon come to an end. He'd noticed that there were fewer mammal bones being found, and his parents were nearly done with excavating the Ceratops skull. Sam and the others had even dug up several ribs, some foot bones, and other parts that they couldn't identify.

"That skull probably weighs a ton," David overheard Sam say to Mr. Hatcher one day. "We need all the help we can get."

David ran to the site. There were several new men standing around with their mules. Mr. Hatcher was hovering over the frill section of the skull.

"Are we raising the Ceratops from the ground today?" David asked eagerly.

Mr. Hatcher climbed out of the patch, clutching his left hand as if it hurt. "It'll take several days to complete. We must be extra cautious so as not to damage it."

"Is this the first full skull to be found?" David couldn't contain his excitement.

"Actually, a man named George Cannon found pieces of a skull in Denver last year," Mr. Hatcher said. "Several months ago, another man named Charles Guernsey showed me a skull of a Ceratops just off his property. But by the time I arrived, they'd broken the skull into pieces. By accident, of course. They didn't know what they had."

"Which is why this one is so special then," David added.

Mr. Hatcher pointed to a thick bone. It was as wide as his hand. "This vertebra is part of the dinosaur's back. It must have been huge, like Guernsey's specimen. That one was named *Ceratops horridus* at first. But when Marsh saw the third horn, he gave the creature the new name *Triceratops*—because it has three horns."

"So, this skull here is a . . . Triceratops?" David was careful to pronounce the new word.

"That's right," Mr. Hatcher said. Then he tipped his hat to David and waved Sam and all the workers over. He gave them instructions on how to raise the skull.

"We need to begin by pedestalling," he said. "You'll dig all around the skull, including beneath it, to keep it from cracking." He drew them a picture of how he wanted them to dig deep beneath the fossil, and wide around it. The skull would be cushioned by a lot of rock and sand. "It should look like a huge mushroom-shaped block with a thick stem by the time you're done."

The men worked long hours for days to prepare the skull to be lifted out. The sun seemed to shine extra hot, making the work even harder. As they worked, everyone dripped with sweat. Their faces were red from exertion.

David's job was to prepare a lot of flour paste and to cut up more burlap sacks. He also had to lay newspapers out on the ground. The workers wet the newspapers and covered the fossil. This would keep the Ceratops skull separated from the flour paste and burlap. It acted as an extra cushion of protection.

David watched as the workers layered the burlap and flour paste over the newspapers. They had to get some under the skull as well. His parents were helping to lay pieces of wood on top of the entire bundle too. He heard his mother say that this helped to reinforce the protection around the fossil.

The next day, the larger men were asked to cut a trench all around the skull. Then, the

other workers placed wood boards underneath and used the burlap and paste to complete the protection of the Ceratops. When they were done, they left it all to dry and harden.

On the day they planned to remove the skull, David watched intently as the men placed ropes all around the lump of rock, plaster, wood, and fossil. They attached the ropes to their mules, which would soon pull the gigantic load out of the ground.

As the mules were being prepared, David went for a water break. He kept his eyes on the men working as he gulped his cup of water. Fascinated by the size of the dig, he stepped a little too close to the edge of the patch. He felt his foot slip, followed by his body. He couldn't stop himself.

He was headed straight for the wrapped Triceratops!

Chapter Five

Time to Go

"No!" David heard many people yell. His mother screamed. As he tumbled, he dug his hands into the sand to stop himself from slamming into the fossil, but it was no use. Just as his foot was inches away from doing damage to the dig, his hand hooked onto a rock that jutted out from the ground. He slid to a sudden stop.

"Phew!" He couldn't imagine what would happen if he'd broken anything.

"Get out of there!" Mr. Hatcher yelled.

David's heart raced as he clambered back up the side of the patch. As he reached the top where the land was flat, he tugged at the leg of a bench to help himself to stand. Then he swung around to show everyone below that he was all right. As he did, he lost his balance and fell into an object behind him. It was the can that he'd packed the day before.

Out spilled hundreds of tiny bones and teeth!

"Oh no!" David cried. "What have I done?"

Everyone froze. Mr. Hatcher and Sam came over to David as he scrambled to pick up the scattered pieces of bone and teeth.

"I'm so sorry," David cried. He was sure his family would be sent packing. "I'll pick them all up and re-sort them. Please don't fire us!"

Mr. Hatcher just shook his head. "I don't have time for this," he said, turning back to the bigger job below. "You deal with it, Sam."

"That was careless," Sam said. "But you will have to fix it. You're lucky the fossil was well protected and no harm was done. Well, except for this." He pointed to the bones all over the ground.

Tears filled David's eyes as he crawled around looking for the bones he had packed so neatly the day before. He had almost cost his parents their jobs. And he had disappointed Mr. Hatcher, whom he had wanted to impress.

David spent the next several hours fixing the mess he'd made. He didn't even dare to stop to watch the mules as they pulled the fossil out of the ground.

When he did finally look again, the large cushion of rock and skull was lying on higher ground. The dig site looked like a deep, empty well, and the mules were worn out.

The workers applauded. David's parents, exhausted but thrilled, waved him over.

"Look at our dragon," his mother said, wiping the sweat off her face with her sleeve.

"I never imagined a dinosaur would be this big," his father said, gulping water. "And this was just the head!"

"I wish I could've seen such an animal when it was alive," David said. "It would've been amazing."

"It most certainly would have," Mr. Hatcher said from behind David. The paleontologist actually looked happy.

It took another day for the workers to ready the skull to be shipped across the country. By that time, David had completed his job too. He'd found all the tiny bones and teeth and packed them back exactly where they belonged. He didn't dare speak to Mr. Hatcher or Sam until he was done.

The men loaded everything onto an extra-large wagon, and six horses pulled their treasures into town for shipping to the museum back east.

That night, everyone who had worked so hard on the dinosaur skull celebrated. They brought whatever food and drink they had and shared it all around.

David and his parents stayed at the dig site for the next several months. In that time, three more complete Triceratops skulls were found. They were carefully packed up and sent to Mr. Hatcher's boss, O. C. Marsh.

Mr. Hatcher traveled back and forth from camp to town. On some trips, David's father would go with him. When they returned, his father would tell him about how Mr. Hatcher was frustrated that Marsh was taking so long to send money to pay the workers.

David's parents weren't paid much, but since they lived in the tents, they didn't need a lot. Still, on the days when Mr. Hatcher finally received money to pay his workers, everyone was cheerful.

By the time winter rolled around, there was little left to dig for in the area. The camp broke up, and people headed back to their homes. Mr. Hatcher was going back to Yale to see his boss, and Sam was going with him.

"I hope you've learned some good lessons here, young man," Mr. Hatcher said to David on their last night at the dig site.

"Indeed, I have, sir," David said. "I knew nothing about dinosaurs before we arrived. They're my favorite animal now."

"Where are you headed next?" Mr. Hatcher asked.

"We're going to follow the next shipment of fossils," David said. "We've saved up enough money to catch the train to New York. My father has relatives who live out there. What about you, sir?"

Mr. Hatcher rubbed his chin. "Me? I've always dreamed of going to Patagonia." Then he laughed and ruffled David's hair. "New York, huh? That's a pretty long journey, but I hear it's friendlier back east. I wish you all the best of luck."

The Wong family hopped onto the back of one of the wagons carrying Mr. Hatcher's final shipment from the dig site. David remembered that first day, when the men who shared the wagon would barely look at them. Now, they chatted happily, like old friends, all the way to the train station. How he would miss them all.

David knew he'd never forget the amazing adventures he'd had, and the friends he'd made at Lance Creek, Wyoming.

"You know," he said to his parents as the wagon trundled along the path, "maybe when I grow up, I'll be a paleontologist. Do you think I'd be allowed to?"

"I believe life will get better for us," his mother said as she wrapped her arm around her son. "You'll be able to become whatever you want."

"The little dragon will grow up to find giant dragons then," his father said with a smile.

"Yes, exactly," said David. "And then I will be able to teach others about dinosaurs and get to name a few. Maybe I'll give one a Chinese name. And maybe, one day, I'll be as famous as John Bell Hatcher, the great dinosaur hunter."

THE HISTORY BEHIND JOHN BELL HATCHER AND HIS DISCOVERY

John Bell Hatcher was born on October 11, 1861, in Cooperstown, Illinois. As a child, he preferred to read while his friends played sports. He was often sick, and people thought he suffered from rheumatism. Today, it is believed he may have had "brittle bone disease," which would have made regular daily activities difficult for him.

Hatcher's love for learning took him all the way to Yale University, one of the best colleges in the country. He studied history, geology, mineralogy, and botany, among other subjects. He paid for college by working as a coal miner. While working as a miner, he also discovered fossils. When he graduated, he became an assistant to O. C. Marsh, a paleontologist from Yale.

Marsh sent Hatcher all over the country to look for fossils. Hatcher turned out to be very good at his job. He had an instinct for reading the land and finding fossils. He invented the anthill method as well as the grid system of labeling fossils. He also found Triceratops and Torosaurus.

Although Marsh gave him credit for the finds, he didn't allow Hatcher to name the dinosaurs. Marsh did that himself and became famous for it. Hatcher also found it difficult to work for Marsh and often had to ask him for money to keep up the work.

The Triceratops skull that Hatcher found in 1889 was 8 feet (2.5 meters) in length. Its three horns and the bony frill were all found intact. After discovering it, Hatcher stopped working for Marsh. He went on to work for Princeton University and continued to collect fossils in South Dakota, Nebraska, and other areas in Wyoming.

Later, Hatcher went on three famous expeditions to Patagonia. He risked everything for these trips, but they paid off. He collected a large number of fossils. These became a huge part of the Princeton University paleontology collection.

On July 3, 1904, Hatcher died of typhoid fever. He was survived by his wife and four children. He was buried in an unmarked grave in Pittsburgh, Pennsylvania. This was a terrible mistake that was fixed in 1995. Now he is remembered as a great paleontologist.

In 1905, a complete Triceratops went on display at the Smithsonian National Museum of Natural History. It was the first and only complete Triceratops to be put on public display, and it was named "Hatcher," in honor of John Bell Hatcher.

The bones that made up Hatcher the Triceratops were actually taken from ten different Triceratops bodies, since no complete Triceratops has ever been unearthed. However, the combination of several individuals did not create the best-looking dinosaur. A *Smithsonian* magazine article on Hatcher the Triceratops put it this way:

"The resulting specimen was a mashup of its fossil donors. Hatcher's skull was too small for his body, his front legs were of different lengths, and his rear feet belonged to an entirely different species with the wrong number of toes."

Hatcher the Triceratops remained on display for more than 90 years. But in 1996, it began to fall apart. Scientists discovered that the Triceratops's bones were rotting from the inside. They quickly took the display down and worked to repair the bones. In its place scientists put up a replica of the Triceratops with the properly proportioned head and feet from the right animal.

Finally, in 2019, Hatcher the Triceratops was put on display once again. This time, though, it was placed into the mouth of a Tyrannosaurus rex. The new display shows the T-Rex biting down on the Triceratops. Even in "death," Hatcher the Triceratops continues to amaze visitors. And it is a wonderful reminder of the great dinosaur hunter, John Bell Hatcher.

GLOSSARY

botany (BOT-a-nee)—the study of plants

burlap (BUR-lap)—a coarse fabric used for bagging or wrapping heavy items

excavate (EK-skuh-vayt)—to dig in the earth

expedition (EK-spuh-di-shuh)—a journey made for a specific purpose

foreigner (FOR-uhn-uhr)—a person from another country

fossil (FAH-suhl)—the remains or traces of an animal or a plant, preserved as rock

frill (FRIL)—a bony collar that fans out around an animal's neck

geology (jee-AHL-uh-jee)—the study of minerals, rocks, and soil

grid (GRID)—a pattern of evenly spaced, parallel lines that cross

ingenious (in-JEEN-yuhss)—inventive and original

mammal (MAM-uhl)—a warm–blooded animal that breathes air; mammals have hair or fur; female mammals feed milk to their young

mineral (MIN-ur-uhl)—a substance found in nature that is not made by a plant or animal and forms the building blocks of rocks

mineralogy (min-ur-AWL-uh-gee)—the study of minerals

paleontologist (pay-lee-uhn-TOL-uh-jist)—a scientist who studies fossils

pedestalling (PED-eh-stall-ing)—a technique used while excavating a fossil that leaves the remains embedded in a cushion of protective soil

replica (REP-luh-kuh)—an exact copy of something

rheumatism (ROO-muh-tiz-uhm)—a disease that causes the joints and muscles to become swollen, stiff, and painful

sediment (SED-uh-muhnt)—a mixture of tiny bits of rock, shells, plants, sand, and minerals

silt (SILT)—sedimentary material consisting of very fine particles

species (SPEE-sheez)—a group of animals with similar features

specimen (SPESS-uh-muhn)—a sample that a scientist studies closely

typhoid fever (TYE-foid FEE-vur)—a serious infectious disease with symptoms of high fever and diarrhea that sometimes leads to death

vertebra (VUR-tuh-bra)—a small bone that surrounds and protects the spinal cord

ACTIVITY

Make Your Own Dinosaur Dig

Build a dinosaur dig site and then excavate your own artifacts!

What You Need:

- 1¼ cups of plaster of paris
- ¾ cup water
- shoebox
- plastic wrap
- plastic toy dinosaurs, colorful rocks, or marbles
- excavation tools, such as a small hammer, paintbrush, old toothbrush, screwdriver, chisel, craft stick, or plastic spoon

What You Do:

Step 1. Make the plaster of paris mixture with water. (Check the box for directions.)

Step 2. Line the inside of the shoebox with plastic wrap.

Step 3. Pour half of the plaster mixture into the shoebox.

Step 4. Press toy dinosaurs, rocks, or marbles into the mixture. Layer more plaster mixture on top.

Step 5. Let the plaster set.

Step 6. When the plaster is set, pop it out of the container.

Step 7. Use the tools to excavate the dinosaurs and other objects from your plaster "dig site."

ABOUT THE AUTHOR

photo by Ailynn Collins

Ailynn Collins is the author of several books, mostly about her favorite subjects—outer space and aliens. She holds a master's degree in writing for children and young adults from Hamline University. She's lived all over the world and speaks six languages. When she's not writing, she's competing in dog sports with one of her five dogs, or showing them in dog shows.

ABOUT THE ILLUSTRATOR

photo by Eva Morales

Eva Morales is a professional Spanish 2D artist and illustrator living near the Mediterranean Sea. She worked in children's publishing, TV, film production, and advertising for about fourteen years. Now she works as a full-time freelance illustrator, using a combination of digital and traditional techniques. Eva loves to walk on the beach and read books in her spare time.